This book belongs to:

....

Note to parents and carers

Read it yourself is a series of classic, traditional tales, written in a simple way to give children a confident and successful start to reading.

Each book is carefully structured to include many high-frequency words that are vital for first reading. The sentences on each page are supported closely by pictures to help with reading, and to offer lively details to talk about.

The books are graded into four levels that progressively introduce wider vocabulary and longer stories as a reader's ability grows.

Ideas for use

- Begin by looking through the book and talking about the pictures. Has your child heard this story before?

- Help your child with any words he does not know, either by helping him to sound them out or supplying them yourself.

- Developing readers can be concentrating so hard on the words that they sometimes don't fully grasp the meaning of what they're reading. Answering the puzzle questions on pages 30 and 31 will help with understanding.

For more information and advice, visit www.ladybird.com/readityourself

Level 1 is ideal for children who have received some initial reading instruction. Each story is told very simply, using a small number of frequently repeated words.

Special features:

Careful match between story and pictures

Opening pages introduce key story words

Large, clear type

Educational Consultant: Geraldine Taylor

A catalogue record for this book is available from the British Library

Published by Ladybird Books Ltd
80 Strand, London, WC2R 0RL
A Penguin Company

004-10 9 8 7 6 5 4
© LADYBIRD BOOKS LTD MMX

ISBN: 978-1-40930-350-3

Printed in China

Goldilocks and the Three Bears

Illustrated by Marina Le Ray

Goldilocks

Mummy Bear

bed

Baby
Bear

Daddy
Bear

chair

porridge

Once upon a time
there were three bears.
And the three bears
loved to eat porridge.

One day the three
bears went for a walk.

"This porridge is too hot," said Goldilocks.

"This porridge is too cold."

"This porridge is just right."

Yum, yum!

"This chair is too hard," said Goldilocks.

"This chair is too soft."

"This chair is just right."

Ooops!

"This bed is too hard," said Goldilocks.

"This bed is too soft."

"Who's been eating my porridge?" said Daddy Bear.

"Who's been eating my porridge?" said Mummy Bear.

"My porridge is all gone,"
said Baby Bear.

20

"Who's been sitting in my chair?" said Daddy Bear.

"Who's been sitting in my chair?" said Mummy Bear.

"My chair is broken,"
said Baby Bear.

"Who's been sleeping in my bed?" said Daddy Bear.

"Who's been sleeping in my bed?" said Mummy Bear.

"Who is sleeping in my bed?"
said Baby Bear.

"Time to go!"
said Goldilocks.

How much do you remember about the story of Goldilocks and the Three Bears? Answer these questions and find out!

- What was wrong with the first chair Goldilocks tried?

- Whose porridge is just right?

- Where do the three bears find Goldilocks?

Look at the pictures from the story and say the order they should go in.

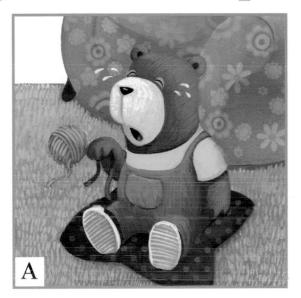

A

B

C

D

Answer: D, C, A, B.

Read it yourself
with Ladybird

The Three Billy Goats Gruff — Level 1

Cinderella — Level 1

Little Red Hen — Level 1

Goldilocks and the Three Bears — Level 1

The Magic Porridge Pot — Level 1

The Ugly Duckling — Level 1

The Gingerbread Man — Level 2

Sleeping Beauty — Level 2

Sly Fox and Red Hen — Level 2

The Three Little Pigs — Level 2

Town Mouse and Country Mouse — Level 2

Little Red Riding Hood — Level 2

The Elves and the Shoemaker — Level 3

Jack and the Beanstalk — Level 3

The Pied Piper of Hamelin — Level 4

The Wizard of Oz — Level 4

Collect all the titles in the series.